SUDHA MURTY

was born in 1950 in Shiggaon, in north Karnataka. She did her MTech in computer science. She is the founder of Infosys Foundation and is currently the chairperson of the Murty Trust. A prolific writer in English and Kannada, she has written novels, technical books, travelogues, collections of short stories and non-fictional pieces, and several bestselling titles for children. Her books have been translated into all the major Indian languages. Sudha Murty is the recipient of the R.K. Narayan Award for Literature. She received the Padma Shri in 2006, the Attimabbe Award from the Government of Karnataka for excellence in Kannada literature in 2011, the Lifetime Achievement Award at the 2018 Crossword Book Awards and the Padma Bhushan in 2023. She has also received ten honorary doctorates. She weaves magical tales and especially enjoys writing for young readers. A generation of children has grown up reading her books, and her stories have been included in textbooks across schools in India.

Dear Reader,
All that glitters is not gold.
Happy Reading!
With affection
Murty

Also in Puffin by SUDHA MURTY

How the Sea Became Salty

How the Onion Got Its Layers

How the Mango Got Its Magic

How the Earth Got Its Beauty

How I Taught My Grandmother to Read and Other Stories

The Magic Drum and Other Favourite Stories

Grandma's Bag of Stories

Grandparents' Bag of Stories

The Bird with Golden Wings

The Magic of the Lost Temple

The Magic of the Lost Story

The Serpent's Revenge: Unusual Tales from the Mahabharata

The Man from the Egg: Unusual Tales about the Trinity

The Upside-Down King: Unusual Tales about Rama and Krishna

The Daughter from a Wishing Tree: Unusual Tales about Women in Mythology

The Sage with Two Horns: Unusual Tales from Mythology

The Sudha Murty Children's Treasury

Unusual Tales from Indian Mythology

How the Bamboo Got its Bounty

Sudha Murty

Illustrations by Pari Satarkar

PUFFIN BOOKS
An imprint of Penguin Random House

PUFFIN BOOKS

USA | Canada | UK | Ireland | Australia
New Zealand | India | South Africa | China | Singapore

Puffin Books is part of the Penguin Random House group of companies
whose addresses can be found at global.penguinrandomhouse.com

Published by Penguin Random House India Pvt. Ltd
4th Floor, Capital Tower 1, MG Road,
Gurugram 122 002, Haryana, India

First published in Puffin Books by Penguin Random House India 2023

10 9 8 7 6 5 4 3 2

ISBN 9780143458197

Typeset in Cormorant
Book design and layout by Samar Bansal
Printed at Thomson Press India Ltd, New Delhi

www.penguin.co.in

To all the trees, all over the world . . .

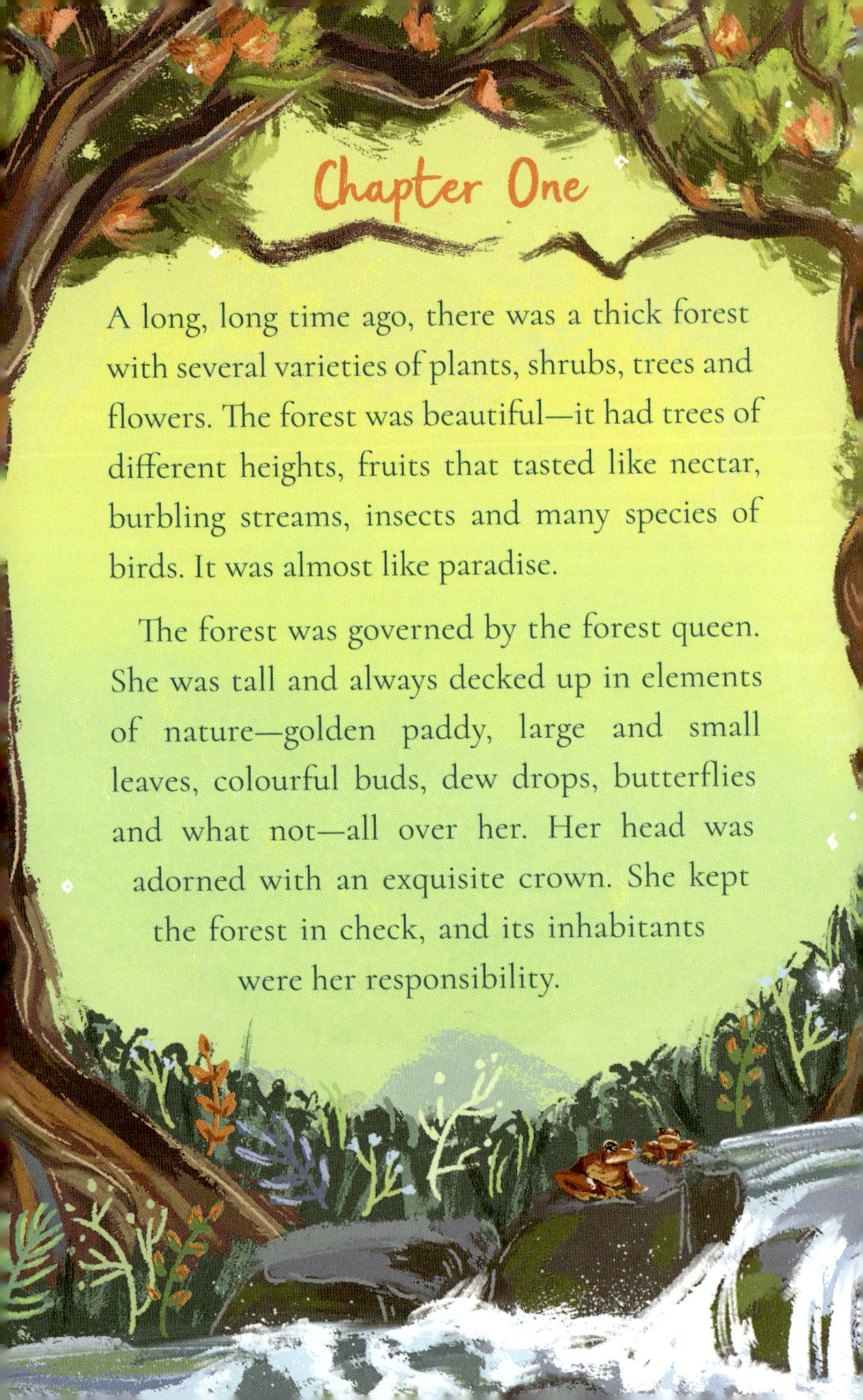

Chapter One

A long, long time ago, there was a thick forest with several varieties of plants, shrubs, trees and flowers. The forest was beautiful—it had trees of different heights, fruits that tasted like nectar, burbling streams, insects and many species of birds. It was almost like paradise.

The forest was governed by the forest queen. She was tall and always decked up in elements of nature—golden paddy, large and small leaves, colourful buds, dew drops, butterflies and what not—all over her. Her head was adorned with an exquisite crown. She kept the forest in check, and its inhabitants were her responsibility.

One day, she sent her messenger, Mr Wind, to the forest.

Whooosh!

Mr Wind came with great force and announced, 'Hello, plants, trees, shrubs and bushes. I come bearing great news; please listen to me! Our queen has sent me to inform you that she is going to visit the forest on the third day of the next month. Since she will be visiting after a long time, we should welcome her with great honour and affection. I request that you prepare to greet her.'

With that, the gush of wind disappeared. There was a loud cheer, and everyone looked forward to the visit.

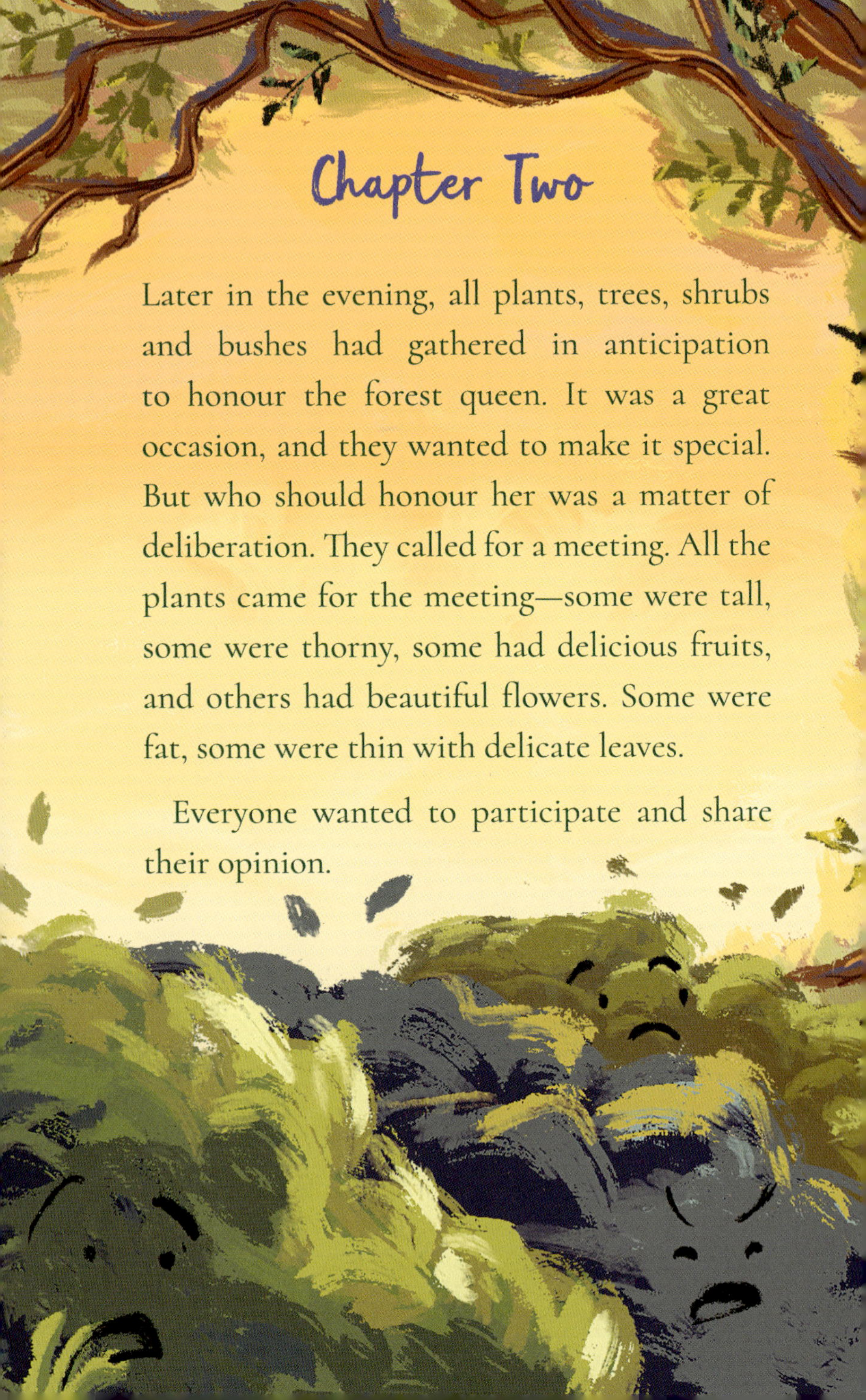

Chapter Two

Later in the evening, all plants, trees, shrubs and bushes had gathered in anticipation to honour the forest queen. It was a great occasion, and they wanted to make it special. But who should honour her was a matter of deliberation. They called for a meeting. All the plants came for the meeting—some were tall, some were thorny, some had delicious fruits, and others had beautiful flowers. Some were fat, some were thin with delicate leaves.

Everyone wanted to participate and share their opinion.

First spoke the **NEEM** tree: 'I think I should have the honour of welcoming the queen because I give shelter to people during hot summer afternoons. My shade is loved by everyone. I also give neem oil which is used to kill germs. I am the most helpful tree among all. Therefore, I deserve this opportunity.'

There was a lot of noise and ruckus in the gathering.

Some small shrubs bowed down in agreement, some trees stood neutral, but the majority of them murmured in disagreement.

The **MANGO** tree roared with laughter. 'Oh, Neem tree, look at you talking about your greatness! Nobody, not even the birds, taste your fruits—they are so bitter. How can someone as bitter as you deserve this honour?

‘Look at my fruits; they are so delicious and have a beautiful colour. My fruits are known to have the nectar of the Earth. In some places, my leaves are used for auspicious occasions. My name appears in the old literature of our country. I am the king of fruits, and I deserve this honour,’ boasted the Mango tree.

'Hahahaha!'

A loud laugh rumbled from up above. All heads looked up. It was the tall **COCONUT** tree.

'What an irony! Once a year you produce your fruits, that too only for three months . . . rest of the time you are of no use.

'Look at me! Every part of my body is useful. A coconut is essential for cooking. I am offered to the mightiest of gods in the temples of our country, and the most useful jute is prepared from my bark. My leaves are used as mats. I also have a nickname of a wishing tree or *kalpataru*. Since I fulfil so many purposes, I am the most suitable for this honour.'

'CHUCKLE! CHUCKLE!'

It was the **TEAK** tree. 'Of all the trees, I am most respected by humans. I sacrifice my life to give excellent wood to human beings. Palaces and homes are built, supported and protected by my wood. I am commercially very useful. Therefore, I deserve the honour.'

'GRRR!'

Slowly, a voice was heard, 'Children, I am the most ancient tree. Travellers seek refuge under my shade, and my fruits are eaten by the birds. I provide a home to so many insects, birds and reptiles. And that is why in all villages and cities I exist,' said the **BANYAN** tree.

There was a murmur in the audience. All trees were in disagreement with each other, and a meek voice was heard in the audience: 'May I speak?'

They all turned and looked in that direction.

There was a small **BAMBOO** tree.

All the old senior trees were very upset. They shouted at the Bamboo tree: 'How dare you speak in front of us? After all, you are the smallest tree—what power do you have? You keep quiet and speak only when spoken to.'

The Bamboo tree kept quiet.

The meeting was adjourned with the conclusion that all trees will showcase their offerings upon the queen's arrival, and the decision will rest with the queen.

Chapter Three

As planned on a pleasant morning, the trees of the forest were fresh and ready with their offerings.

Soon the queen arrived. She looked beautiful with her lush hair adorned with leaves and flowers and her exquisite crown. The birds started chirping on her arrival, the stream broke into a meditative song with its gentle gurgles, and the many plants and trees swayed cheerfully in unison as they received her. They all joined together, as planned, to give her a special and warm welcome. The queen was delighted.

Mr Wind, after a short while, blew past, and a gentle breeze took over.

There was silence. The queen began to speak:

'My wonderful, giving and loving creatures, I am so pleased to meet you all today. I must start by telling you that I went on a tour around cities, towns and villages. It was such a joy to see the beauty of our Earth.

'This visit really moved my heart, and I thought I'd come back and present a reward to a tree who I learnt to be the most useful to the common man; it's the most unassuming tree.'

There was loud cheering in the audience. Excited, all the trees hooted and tried to guess what the reward could be. And most importantly, who would get it.

'First of all, I must appreciate everything you do for Mother Earth. The flowers that bring vibrant colours and sweet smells. Our lush green trees that offer so much—fuel, food, fruits, nuts, shade and shelter. They are so crucial to the environment as they are the major source of oxygen for all living beings. Without trees, we couldn't survive.

'So I thought I would reward a tree today, based on my observations during this trip.'

As soon as the queen said this, there was complete chaos.

All the old trees started recalling their qualities. They spoke over each other, often cutting the other, but the queen heard all of them patiently and smiled. She did not give any judgement.

The queen also took her time to gaze around the forest, walking amidst the gorgeous trees, touching the creepers, smelling the fragrance of flowers, and tasting some of the juiciest fruits out there.

Her eyes eventually laid on the Bamboo tree at one end of the forest, standing silently and solemnly. The queen smiled and moved on.

She then took her seat on a giant throne made of beautiful creepers and climbing roses.

She clapped her hands to get everyone's attention and continued, 'Like I said, I admire all the bountiful trees, but during my tour, I noticed one tree that gives unconditional service to humankind. In my opinion, it doesn't matter how tall we stand, how beautiful we look or how popular we are.'

Gently and with a lot of wisdom, the queen went on. 'While all trees have my equal respect, I can grant this reward to the one and only Bamboo.'

'OOOHHHH!'

Went all the trees.

Chapter Four

With a firm voice, the queen continued, 'The Bamboo takes several forms—when a child is born, the Bamboo becomes its cradle; a winnow during harvest; a basket for fruits. For workers, it serves as a ladder. It is also furniture for everyday use, like a cot for one to sleep on. Its tender shoots are vegetables, and people can make houses out of it.

'More than anyone, it was Lord Krishna who was very fond of Bamboo. He produced beautiful music by blowing into a flute made from the Bamboo.

'What impressed me the most is that it can grow anywhere and doesn't require a lot of care—only a handful of mud and rainwater is sufficient for it to grow and multiply. It also grows fast; once it's cut, a shoot grows in no time. It doesn't ask for anything, endures all kinds of weather and most importantly, it serves others in so many ways.

'From human birth to death, our Bamboo finds one way or another to be useful to a common person. It is truly the unsung and the forgotten.'

Bamboo, who was standing quietly until then, suddenly had all the attention from the fellow inhabitants of the forest.

Too shy to speak, Bamboo mildly uttered, 'Your Majesty, I am grateful for your acknowledgement, and in return, I only ask for continuous support for my tree and plant family.'

The queen smiled.

'Oh, Bamboo, I'm touched by your words.'

This made all the trees think hard; they all looked solemn.

'You help human beings in innumerable ways, and that is why, Bamboo, I want to grant you a blessing: let there be a thousand varieties of bamboo across the world, so that you are available to as many people as possible. May you grow in as many different climates as possible,' concluded the queen.

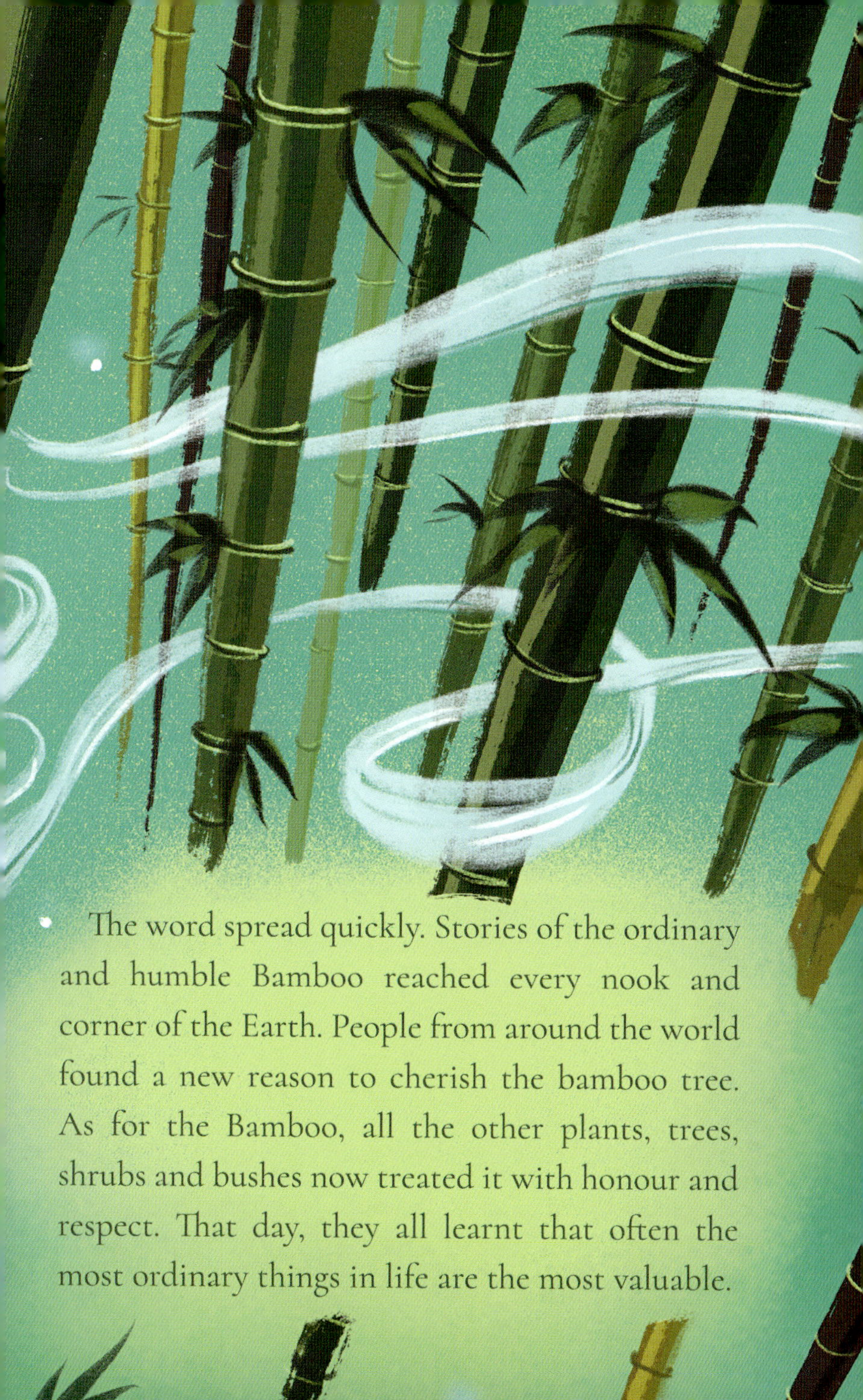

The word spread quickly. Stories of the ordinary and humble Bamboo reached every nook and corner of the Earth. People from around the world found a new reason to cherish the bamboo tree. As for the Bamboo, all the other plants, trees, shrubs and bushes now treated it with honour and respect. That day, they all learnt that often the most ordinary things in life are the most valuable.

Acknowledgements

I would like to thank Sohini Mitra, my young editor Simran Kaur, and the illustrator Pari Satarkar.

I would also like to thankfully acknowledge all the children who read and enjoy my books.

PARI SATARKAR

Pari Satarkar, a Pune-based animator and illustrator, set out on the winding paths of visual art in pursuit of a lifelong passion for storytelling. These paths have guided her through a world of colours, strokes and movement. Her work reflects an earnest fascination with the natural world, often manifested through whimsical animals and flowers adorning the margins of books.

Her work can be found on Instagram at pari.jpeg.

Scan QR code to access the
Penguin Random House India website